# Zoe's Rescue Zoo

## The Talkative Tiger

*Amelia Cobb*

Illustrated by
**Sophy Williams**

nosy
crow

## With special thanks to Siobhan Curham

*For John Arthur*

First published in the UK in 2021 by Nosy Crow Ltd
The Crow's Nest, 14 Baden Place
Crosby Row, London SE1 1YW

www.nosycrow.com

ISBN: 978 1 78800 935 5

Nosy Crow and associated logos are trademarks and/or
registered trademarks of Nosy Crow Ltd

Text copyright © Working Partners Ltd, 2021
Illustrations © Sophy Williams, 2021

A CIP catalogue record for this book will be available from the British Library

Printed and bound in Great Britain by Clays Ltd, Elcograf S.p.A.

Papers used by Nosy Crow are made from wood grown in sustainable forests.

MIX
Paper from
responsible sources
FSC® C018072

1 3 5 7 9 10 8 6 4 2

# Chapter One
## A New Arrival

Zoe Parker took a fish from her bucket and threw it into the water. It was breakfast time at the Rescue Zoo where she lived, and Zoe was helping to feed the sea otters. Sasha, one of the youngest sea otters, caught the fish in her front paws and started to eat. Sasha's brother and sister, Alex and Nina, whistled happily as

Zoe threw more fish into the water for them.

*Someone* wasn't excited though.

"Yuck, yuck, yuck!" said Zoe's pet mouse lemur, Meep.

Zoe was able to understand what Meep was saying because Zoe had a special secret. She was able to talk to animals and understand what they were saying. No-one else knew her secret, not even her mum or her Great-Uncle Horace. "What's wrong?" she asked, crouching down beside Meep.

"Fish for breakfast!" Meep wrinkled his tiny black nose.

"Don't worry," Zoe smiled. "I have something I know you'll like." She took a banana from the pocket of her shorts, peeled it, and handed it to Meep.

"Yum, yum, yum!" exclaimed Meep, before taking a bite.

Zoe looked back at the pool. Three sea otters were floating on their backs eating their fish, their wet coats glistening in the summer sunshine.

"How are you getting on, Zoe?" Jess, the sea otters' keeper, called as she came into the enclosure.

"Great!" replied Zoe. "They're really enjoying their fish."

"They certainly seem happy," said Jess as the sea otters gave a contented cooing sound. "But are you sure you don't mind working on the first day of your summer holiday?"

"No, it's fun!" Zoe wanted to be a zookeeper when she grew up, and she loved helping with the animals whenever she could.

"It looks as if we'll be needing your help," said Jess, nodding to the empty enclosure next door. "I wonder who our new arrival will be."

Zoe looked at the enclosure. Her Great-Uncle Horace, who owned the Rescue Zoo, had recently had a beautiful new habitat built. There was a pond in the middle, with rocks and trees all around it. "It must be something that needs a lot of space and likes to climb and swim," said Zoe. "Maybe it's a crocodile!"

"Could be. Or maybe it's a family of apes," said Jess, throwing more fish into the water.

Zoe nodded.

A cheery BEEP BEEP BEEP rang out around the zoo. Great-Uncle Horace's convertible car drove through the zoo gates. The car's top was down and Great-Uncle Horace was wearing a hat to shield his face from the sun. A small trailer was attached to the back of the convertible car, holding a large crate. Zoe's heart pounded with excitement. It must be the new animal! The elephants in the enclosure nearby began to trumpet cheerily. The monkeys began to shriek with excitement. Meep ran round in circles waving his paws. All of the animals loved Great-Uncle Horace because he'd rescued them and brought them to live in the zoo.

Zoe put down her bucket and raced

from the otters' enclosure. Meep and Jess
followed close behind. Several of the other
keepers and Zoe's mum, Lucy, who was
the zoo vet, were also hurrying over.

"Great-Uncle Horace, it's so good to see
you!" cried Zoe. "Do you have the new
animal? Who have you

rescued this time?"

"Good morning, Zoe," called Great-Uncle Horace, as he got out of the car. There was a flutter of wings and a beautiful bright blue bird flew out and perched on his shoulder. It was Kiki, Great-Uncle Horace's hyacinth macaw, who went everywhere with him.

"Can some of you help me with this crate?" Great-Uncle Horace asked the keepers.

Zoe watched as Great-Uncle Horace, Mark, the big cat keeper, and Mr Pinch, the zoo manager, carefully lowered the crate right in front of the new enclosure. Great-Uncle Horace opened the enclosure gate. Then he opened the crate. A blur of orange, white and black stripy fur raced into the enclosure.

"What is it?" chattered Meep, climbing on to Zoe's shoulder to get a better view. The blur of stripy fur clambered up the rocks then sat still for a moment, looking this way and that.

"It's a tiger cub!" cried Zoe.

Everyone laughed and cheered as the tiger cub bounced around the enclosure

and splashed into the pool. Everyone
apart from Mr Pinch.

"Look at the mess it's making, splashing
water everywhere," he said with a sigh.
Mr Pinch always wanted everything to be
neat and tidy.

"Tigers love to swim, Mr Pinch," said
Mark. "They can swim up to twenty-nine
kilometres a day."

"Wow!" exclaimed Zoe. "So that's why he's got his own pond."

"Why on earth would tigers want to do that?" Mr Pinch frowned and shook his head.

"It sounds like tigers love water just as much as sea otters do," chuckled Jess.

The cub got out of the water and scampered up the rocks. He yelped happily as he climbed higher.

"Looks like tigers love to climb too," giggled Zoe.

"And leap." Mark laughed as the cub jumped from one rock to the next.

"What's the tiger saying?" Meep whispered in Zoe's ear, as the cub continued to yelp.

"He's saying he's really happy to be here," Zoe whispered back. "Where did you rescue him from, Great-Uncle Horace?"

"From a place called Bengal in India," replied Great-Uncle Horace. "Unfortunately, the forest he was born in has been turned into farmland. When his mother died, he had nowhere to live."

"That's really sad," said Zoe, frowning.

"It's OK, love, he's safe now," said Lucy, giving her a hug.

"A hundred years ago there were forty thousand tigers in the forests of Bengal," continued Great-Uncle Horace. "But now there are only one thousand four hundred."

"But why?" asked Zoe.

"Because people keep taking the land away. And it's not just happening to tigers." Great-Uncle Horace stroked Kiki's bright blue feathers. "Even hyacinth macaws and mouse lemurs are losing their habitats in the wild."

"Yikes!" yelped Meep, flinging his paws around Zoe's neck.

"That's terrible," said Zoe. She hated thinking of animals losing their homes. Surely there was something they could do to help.

## Chapter Two
# Too Many Questions

"Don't worry, Zoe," said Lucy. "I'm sure the tiger cub will be very happy in his new home."

*But what about all of the other animals who are losing their homes?* Zoe thought. Great-Uncle Horace couldn't rescue them all.

"I'll be back to give him his check-up later, Uncle Horace," said Lucy. "I just need to give the patients in the zoo hospital their breakfast."

"I say we get some enrichment toys for our new arrival," said Great-Uncle Horace to Mark. "To help him feel more at home."

"Can I look after him while you're gone?" asked Zoe.

Great-Uncle Horace looked thoughtful for a moment. "As long as he's OK with it. Tigers can be very territorial, even when they're cubs. They like their own space."

"Of course," said Zoe. She went over to the enclosure gate and crouched down. As soon as he saw her, the little tiger came racing over. He sniffed at her hand and let out a happy chattering sound.

"Well, it sounds as if he'd very much like

you to take care of him," chuckled Great-Uncle Horace.

Zoe beamed with pride as she felt for the paw-shaped pendant around her neck. Great-Uncle Horace had given her the pendant as a birthday present. It opened all of the enclosure gates in the zoo. She pressed the silver charm on to a pad beside the gate and it swung open. The tiger cub nuzzled her leg, chatting excitedly.

"Hello!" Zoe crouched down to greet the cub. Meep hopped down from her shoulder. "My name's Zoe and this is Meep. He's a mouse lemur."

The cub snorted happily and rubbed his cheek against hers.

"He says his name is Teddy," Zoe said to Meep.

The cub raced around them
in a circle, continuing to snort.

"He's making me dizzy!" exclaimed
Meep, spinning round and round to try
and keep up with Teddy.

"He's very excited to be here," said Zoe.

16

"We're very excited to have you too."
She stroked the cub's silky head. A second
later he was bounding off again, peering
through the fence into the sea otters'
enclosure. He made a soft growling sound
and looked at Zoe curiously.

"That's the sea otters' enclosure," replied
Zoe. "Great-Uncle Horace rescued them
too. He rescued all of the animals at the
zoo."

The sea otters raised their heads from
the water and cooed hello to Teddy.

Teddy scampered off up the pile of rocks
and looked into the enclosure on the
other side, yowling loudly to say hello.

"That's where the elephants live," replied
Zoe.

Bertie the elephant gave a cheery
trumpet hello.

Teddy came bounding back over, still talking.

"I like his stripy fur," said Meep.

Teddy chattered some more.

"He says that no two tigers have exactly the same stripes. He thinks his are very pretty," Zoe said. "I think so, too." She heard the sound of voices. Visitors were starting to come through the zoo gates. "You're going to see a lot of people now," she explained to Teddy. She hoped he wouldn't be scared. But Teddy didn't seem scared at all. He scampered over to the fence, chattering loudly as a boy and girl came running over.

"Look! Look! It's a tiger cub," the boy exclaimed.

Teddy yelped at Zoe.

"He wants to know if they're brother

and sister," Zoe explained to Meep. "I think they must be," Zoe whispered to the cub. "They both have the same red hair."

"Look, Mum, it's a tiger cub!" said the girl as a woman came over to join them.

"Ah, isn't he sweet," said the mum.

Teddy ran round in a circle chasing his tail, chattering louder than ever.

"I don't know who their mum's favourite animal is," replied Zoe.

The woman smiled as Teddy rolled on his back on the ground.

"I think she likes tigers best now she's seen you!" giggled Zoe.

Just then Great-Uncle Horace and Mark returned with armfuls of toys. As they came into the enclosure Teddy bounded over to greet them.

"Well, well, someone looks very happy in his new home," said Great-Uncle Horace. "Good work, Zoe. Have you come up with a name for him?"

"Yes. His name is Teddy." Zoe smiled to herself. If only Great-Uncle Horace knew that she didn't come up with the animals' names at all. The animals told them to her!

Mark placed a barrel on its side on the ground. "Teddy can have fun rolling this," he explained to Zoe.

"And he can have fun chewing on this." Great-Uncle Horace took a thick piece of rope from the box he was holding. "And chasing this." He took out a large ball.

But instead of playing with the toys, Teddy leaped inside the box.

"Looks like he prefers the box," giggled Zoe.

More people started gathering outside the enclosure, watching Teddy play.

"I love his stripes," called out a little boy.

"Did you know that no two tigers have exactly the same pattern of stripes?" said Zoe.

"Wow, that's really cool," replied the boy.

"Where's he from?" asked a woman.

"A place called Bengal," replied Zoe.

More and more people gathered by the enclosure. And now, instead of looking at Teddy, they were all staring at her. Zoe's face started to flush.

"What does he like to eat?" another man asked.

"Oh – I – um – I'm not sure," stammered Zoe.

"How old is he?" another woman called.

"I don't know," Zoe's face was burning

now, she felt so embarrassed.

Great-Uncle Horace came over and placed a hand on her shoulder. "Young Teddy is about four months old," he told the woman. "So he won't be this size forever. Tigers are the largest wild cats in the world. They can grow up to three metres long!"

"Wow, that's really long!" a boy gasped. "What do they like to eat?"

"Tigers are carnivores, so they only eat meat." Great-Uncle Horace turned to Zoe and smiled. "And talking of food, how about we join your mum for lunch in the café while Teddy plays with his new toys?"

Meep's long tail sprang up with excitement at the mention of food.

"That would be great." Zoe went over and patted Teddy on the head. "Have fun with your toys," she whispered. "I'll be back to see you soon."

As she followed Great-Uncle Horace out of the enclosure, she gave a relieved sigh. She loved being with the animals but having to answer so many questions from so many people was a little scary!

# Chapter Three
# A Table for Lunch

Zoe followed Great-Uncle Horace into
the zoo café with Meep perched on her
shoulder. Trays of freshly baked cupcakes
filled the counter. They smelled so
delicious they made Zoe's mouth water.
Meep clapped his front paws, clearly
excited by the smell of food too. As they
went over to the counter Zoe saw the

little boy and girl with the red hair. They were sitting at a table with their mum and dad.

"Look, Mum, there's the girl from the tiger enclosure," cried the boy.

Zoe's face flushed again. She really hoped they wouldn't ask her any more questions while she was trying to eat!

"Hello, Zoe, hello, Mr Higgins," Sally, the café manager, called from behind the counter.

"Hello, Sally." Great-Uncle Horace gave her a cheery grin. "We'd like a table for lunch please."

"Why does he want to eat a table for lunch?" Meep chattered in Zoe's ear, his big golden eyes wide with shock.

"He doesn't want a table to eat!" Zoe whispered, trying not to laugh. "He wants a table to sit at."

"Why didn't he say that then?" chattered Meep.

"Hello, Meep," Sally leaned over the counter and stroked the mouse lemur's soft grey fur. "Would you like some lunch too?"

"Yes, but tell her I don't want a table," Meep muttered to Zoe.

Zoe bit her lip to stop herself laughing. "Yes please," she said to Sally.

They went over to a table in the corner. Meep hopped down from Zoe's shoulder and perched on the back of a chair.

"Aha! Here's your mother," said Great-Uncle Horace as Lucy came into the café. She was carrying her vet's bag and a stethoscope hung around her neck.

"So, how's the new arrival doing?" Lucy

asked as she sat down at the table.

"He's doing really well," said Zoe. "His name's Teddy."

"I don't think I've ever seen such a lively tiger cub." Great-Uncle Horace stroked his white beard thoughtfully. "Maybe we should do something special to celebrate his arrival at the zoo."

Zoe nodded. "Could we do something to let people know that tigers are losing their homes? I really want to help them."

"Maybe we could have a fundraiser to help protect tigers' habitats in the wild?" suggested Lucy.

"That's a wonderful idea," said Great-Uncle Horace.

Zoe looked at Meep, who was gazing hungrily at the food on the counter. "You know, lemurs and other animals are losing their homes too – maybe we could raise money for all of them," she suggested.

"Yes, yes!" said Great-Uncle Horace, clapping his hands and smiling. "I'll ask the keepers to give talks about what's happening to their animals."

"And maybe you could give a talk about how mouse lemurs are losing their homes in the wild too," Lucy said to Zoe.

"That's an excellent idea!" exclaimed
Great-Uncle Horace.

"Oh – uh – I –" stammered Zoe.

"Yes! Yes! Yes!" Meep chattered, waving
his paws.

Zoe got butterflies in her tummy at the
thought of having to give a talk in front
of lots of people. But she didn't want to let
Great-Uncle Horace down. "OK."

"Wonderful!" exclaimed Great-Uncle
Horace. "Now let's have lunch!"

Later that night, Zoe tossed and turned
in her bed. No matter how hard she tried,
she couldn't get to sleep. When she was
little and couldn't sleep, her mum had
told her to close her eyes and picture
sheep jumping over a fence. "If you count

the sheep as they jump, you'll soon fall asleep," Lucy had said.

But now, every time Zoe tried to picture a sheep, she imagined it asking her a question instead of jumping. Soon, there was a whole flock of sheep in her head, all baa-ing questions she couldn't answer. Zoe sat up in bed, her heart pounding. What if she messed up her talk? What if she ran out of things to say? What if she stood there in silence? What if no-one gave any money to help protect the animals' habitats because her talk was so bad? Zoe sighed loudly.

"What's the matter, Zoe?" Meep asked sleepily from where he was curled up at the end of the bed.

"I'm worried about giving my talk. I get really nervous when lots of people are

looking at me."

Meep scampered up the bed and sat in her lap. "Don't be scared. You always have lots of people looking at you when you make that funny sound with your voice."

Zoe frowned. "What funny sound?"

"When you make it go all squeaky, like this…" Meep started making a high-pitched wailing sound.

"Shhh!" Zoe giggled. "You'll wake Mum! When do I ever make that sound?"

"You do it with your friends at school." Meep started wailing again, quieter this time.

"Do you mean singing in the school choir?"

"Yes! You do that in front of lots of people, don't you?"

"But when I'm singing in the choir I have all my friends with me. When I give my talk I'll be all on my own." Zoe's tummy started fluttering again.

"You won't be on your own," Meep said with a yawn. "I'll be with you."

"Thanks, Meep." She kissed the top of his head and lay down. Meep curled next to her on the pillow. As Zoe stroked his silky fur, she finally started falling asleep.

The thought of having Meep with her was comforting. But he wouldn't be able to help if she forgot what to say.

## Chapter Four
# The Stripy Sea Otter

The next morning after breakfast, Zoe hurried back to see Teddy. She couldn't wait to find out how he was settling in. As she and Meep made their way along the winding path into the heart of the zoo, Meep stopped and tilted his head to one side.

"Listen," he said.

"To what?" Zoe looked at him, puzzled. She couldn't hear a thing.

"It's so quiet," replied Meep. "It's never this quiet."

Zoe frowned. Meep was right. Normally, the zoo was full of noise as the animals all woke up. But today the monkeys were still curled up asleep in their trees and there was no sign of life from the elephant enclosure either. Zoe looked over to the sea otter enclosure. Nina, Alex and Sasha were floating on their backs in the water, fast asleep too. Zoe wondered if she'd gotten up too early by accident. But over in the distance, she saw the zoo gates opening to let the first of the visitors in. Why were the animals still asleep?

One of the animals wasn't asleep

though. As they got closer to Teddy's enclosure, she saw a blur of stripy fur and the sound of his chatter broke the silence. He was talking to the trees in his enclosure. Zoe laughed as she heard him tell one of the trees that he was going to call him Mr Leaf Head.

"Hello Teddy," she called, using her paw-print pendant to let herself into the enclosure.

Teddy came racing over, chattering away.

"What's he saying?" asked Meep.

"He's telling us all about what happened last night," replied Zoe. Teddy nuzzled his head against her leg and she knelt down to stroke him. "You saw Mr Silver Face looking down at you?" She frowned.

Teddy nodded and gave a little bark.

"Oh, that's your name for the moon!" Zoe giggled.

Teddy grinned and yelped happily.

"There were silver holes in the sky?" Zoe smiled. "Is that what you call the stars?"

Teddy nodded his stripy head.

Just then Mr Pinch came marching along the path towards them. As usual, his uniform was very smart and his shiny shoes gleamed in the sunlight.

"Uh-oh!" said Meep. Meep didn't like Mr Pinch because he was always grumbling about the animals making a mess.

"Excuse me, sir," called a man standing by the sea otters' enclosure.

"Yes?" replied Mr Pinch.

"I was just wondering why these sea otters are still asleep?" said the man. "I wanted to see them play."

"There's nothing wrong with sleeping animals," replied Mr Pinch. "A sleeping animal is a tidy animal!" And with that he carried on his way.

Bertie the elephant trundled over to the fence between his and Teddy's enclosure.

"Good morning, Bertie," Zoe called.

Normally, Bertie trumpeted cheerily when he saw Zoe but not this morning. His head hung low, his ears flopped beside his face and his trunk trailed on the ground.

"What's the matter?" asked Zoe, going

over to the fence.

Bertie gave a sad little squeak.

"Oh no! Why didn't you get any sleep?"

Bertie gave another squeak and pointed his trunk at Teddy, who was now splashing in and out of his pool.

"Oh dear," said Zoe.

"What's wrong?" asked Meep.

"Bertie didn't get any sleep last night because Teddy wouldn't stop talking. That must be why all the other animals are so sleepy too." Zoe put her hand through the fence and patted Bertie on the trunk. "Don't worry, I'll have a talk with him."

Zoe hurried over to Teddy, who was chatting away to himself by the side of the pool.

"Teddy, Bertie just told me that you were talking a lot last night."

The tiger cub nodded and chattered even faster.

"It's lovely that you're so excited to be here but night-time is meant to be sleep time."

Teddy scampered over to the front of his enclosure and started yowling at the man

42

watching the sea otters.

"What's he saying now?" asked Meep.

"He's saying that he thinks that man looks like a tree and he wants to call him Mr Tree Trunk Legs," giggled Zoe. With the man's brown trousers and green top, she could see what he meant.

Teddy came bounding back and yelped excitedly.

"It's great that you have so many ideas to talk about." Zoe smiled. "But maybe you could not talk about them when the moon and stars are out?"

Teddy nodded and promised, then raced over to the pool and jumped in. Every so often he lifted his head out of the water and called out something.

"I really don't think you've just seen a mermaid," giggled Zoe.

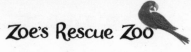

"What's he saying now?" asked Meep as Teddy called over again.

"He wants to know if he looks like a sea otter," explained Zoe. "Yes, a very stripy sea otter," she replied.

*And a very talkative one too!* she thought to herself.

If only Teddy could give her talk –
he'd never run out of things to say! She
checked her watch. Great-Uncle Horace
had called a meeting at his house about
the endangered habitats event and it
was about to start. She picked up Meep
and said goodbye to Teddy. Her stomach
twisted a little as she started to walk.

*I hope I can do a good talk, for Meep and the*
*other mouse lemurs' sake!*

ENDANGERED HABITAT DAY

## Chapter Five
# Practice Makes Perfect

Great-Uncle Horace lived in a big old
house on Higgins Hill, overlooking the
zoo. As Zoe walked up the hill, she saw
some of the zookeepers setting up rows
of chairs in front of the house. A huge
banner had been laid out on the grass.
The words on it read: ENDANGERED
HABITAT DAY. Each letter had been

painted in a different colour of the
rainbow. Normally, Zoe got excited
whenever there was a special event at
the zoo, but not this time. She looked
at the rows of chairs and pictured them
full of people staring at her. Her tummy
churned.

Great-Uncle Horace came hurrying out
of the house with Kiki on his shoulder. He
was holding a clipboard and his round
glasses were perched on the end of his
nose. "Hello, Zoe!" he called. "What do
you think of our presentation space?"

"I think it looks great," replied Zoe.
She could hardly tell him it was one of
the scariest things she'd ever seen! Meep
didn't seem at all worried though as he
scampered around the chairs.

"Are you ready to start work on your

talk?" asked Great-Uncle Horace.

Zoe nodded. "I know some things about mouse lemurs already. They come from an island called Madagascar, off the coast of Africa. They live in forests, and their habitat is in danger of being cut down."

"That's right," said Great-Uncle Horace, looking serious. "It's important to let people know about it. Now, if you would like any more facts, I know there's a book on lemurs in my library."

"Thank you." Zoe hurried down the huge hallway of Great-Uncle Horace's house. Meep raced in behind her and scampered up the bannister of the wide staircase.

"Wheeeeeeeeeee!" he shrieked as he slid back down.

"Come on, Meep," giggled Zoe, "We've

got work to do."

She went through one
of the doorways off
the hall, into
Great-Uncle
Horace's
library.

The tall
walls were
covered with shelves
full of books, all arranged
alphabetically. Sure enough,
there was a book on mouse lemurs
on the shelf of books beginning with
M. Meep jumped up and down with
excitement when he saw the picture of
the mouse lemur on the cover. Zoe took
the book over to a large desk by the

window. She flicked through the pages, writing interesting facts about mouse lemurs in her notepad. Meep hopped up on to the desk and watched her work.

"Did you know that the word lemur means ghost?" she said.

"Why? Am I a ghost?" asked Meep.

"No! It's because lemurs have such big eyes. People thought they looked like ghosts," Zoe grinned.

"Woooooo! I'm a spooky ghost," cried Meep, running around the desk waving his paws.

"Don't try and scare me right now, Meep. I'm already nervous enough!" Zoe glanced out of the window at the rows of chairs on the lawn.

"Sorry," said Meep, scuttling over to nuzzle her.

Zoe hugged him tightly. "That's OK."
She thought of all the mouse lemurs in
Madagascar who had lost their homes.
She had to give her talk, no matter how
scary it felt. She had to do something
to try and help. Zoe looked back at her

notepad and started planning her talk, deciding which facts she should use and which she could leave out.

Once she'd finished, she went back outside. Great-Uncle Horace was helping Mark set up a stall about Teddy and other endangered tigers.

"Hello, Zoe, did you find what you needed?" he asked.

"Yes, thanks."

"I've got a great idea," said Great-Uncle Horace. "Why don't you practise giving your talk to us?"

"Yes, go on, Zoe," said Mark.

Zoe's heart sank. It didn't sound like a great idea to her. It sounded like a really scary idea! But at least she'd only be giving her talk to two people. "OK," she replied, her heart pounding. But before

she could begin Great-Uncle Horace
clapped his hands loudly.

"Attention please!" he called to the
other zookeepers. "Zoe would like to
practise her talk."

"Go Zoe!" cheered Jess as the
zookeepers all sat down on the seats.
Zoe's face flushed red. She looked down
at her notebook and took a deep breath.

"Mouse lemurs are from a place
called Mada-madagascar," she stuttered.
"Madagascar is close to – close to Africa."
The sun suddenly felt very hot and Zoe's
mouth went dry. "The mouse lemur is—"

"Can you speak up a bit?" called
Kieran, the kangaroo keeper.

"Yes, sorry." Zoe tried to raise her voice.
"The mouse lemur is now an endangered
species because – because…" She tried

to turn the page in her notebook and it dropped to the floor.

"I think that maybe Zoe needs a little more time to prepare," said Great-Uncle Horace. "How about we all take a break? I've set up some drinks and snacks in the kitchen, please do help yourselves."

The zookeepers hurried off inside the house.

"Are you OK, Zoe?" asked

Great-Uncle Horace once they'd gone. "I know you know this stuff. You said it to me earlier!"

Zoe nodded. "I just get really nervous when there's so many people looking at me."

"I know it can be scary, but you'll be great." Great-Uncle Horace patted her on the back. "Whenever I feel nervous talking to a big group of people, I just imagine that they've all got bowls of fruit on their heads. Then they're not nearly as scary."

Zoe grinned. She wasn't sure if this would help with her talk though. Picturing her audience with bowls of fruit on their heads would probably make her laugh! Her smile faded. If she laughed, she'd mess up her talk and then no-one would give any money to help the mouse lemurs or the tigers or any of the other endangered species.

She just had to get this right!

## Chapter Six
# Asking for Help

Zoe and Meep headed off down the hill and back into the zoo. Talking to Great-Uncle Horace about being nervous had made her feel a bit better. She wondered if she should ask the animals' advice too. As they reached the meadow at the edge of the zoo, she spotted Cleo the zebra, grazing. Zebras always seemed so calm, maybe she would be able to help Zoe not feel scared. As Zoe approached the fence, Cleo trotted over to greet her.

"Hi Cleo!" Zoe stroked the zebra. "I need your help."

Cleo neighed and Zoe told her all about the talk and how scared she was feeling. "What do you do when you need to feel brave?" she asked.

Cleo gave a gentle whinny.

"You shake?" Zoe stared at her in surprise.

Cleo nodded and then she started shaking her whole body.

Meep burst out laughing. "She looks like a wobbly jelly!"

Cleo gave another whinny.

"Shaking like that helps her get the fear out of her body," explained Zoe.

It did sound like a good idea but Zoe couldn't imagine what would happen if she started shaking like a jelly at her talk! Maybe she ought to ask another animal for help. She patted Cleo goodbye and set off along the path. As the nocturnal house came into view she decided to pop in and see Hugo the hedgehog. He always loved to be helpful.

The nocturnal house was so dark after the bright sunshine outside that it took Zoe a moment to see properly. She went past the bats and Suki the chinchilla until she got to the final enclosure. Hugo was sitting by a log nibbling on a piece of apple. As soon as he saw Zoe and Meep he shuffled over, squeaking excitedly.

"Hello, Hugo," said Zoe. "I was wondering if you could help me." Zoe

explained about feeling nervous about
her talk and Hugo squeaked again.

"What did he say?" asked Meep.

"He says that when he gets scared, he
curls into a ball," replied Zoe.

Hugo rolled up tightly until his face
disappeared and he was a ball of spikes.
Then he poked his nose out and squeaked
hopefully.

"Yes, that was very helpful, Hugo," replied Zoe. But although she'd love to curl up in a ball to hide from her audience, she'd never be able to give her talk like that. She wouldn't have any spikes to protect her either!

They said good-bye to Hugo and went back out into the sunshine.

"Who are you going to ask next?" asked Meep.

"I think I'll ask Bertie," said Zoe. Elephants were so big and strong, surely he'd be able to help her.

When they got to the elephant enclosure, Bertie still looked really tired. Zoe explained why she needed his help. Bertie flicked up his trunk and trumpeted loudly.

Meep shrieked and covered his ears

with his paws.

"He says that trumpeting loudly always makes him feel better," explained Zoe.

"Well, it makes my ears feel sore!" muttered Meep.

"Thanks, Bertie," said Zoe. But she wasn't sure if yelling her talk at the top of her voice would really help. She didn't want to give her audience sore ears! Then she heard Teddy chattering away to himself in his enclosure.

"Let's ask Teddy," she said to Meep. "Tigers are so brave, I'm sure he'll have something to say."

"He always has something to say!" chuckled Meep.

As Zoe used her pendant to enter the enclosure, Teddy came bounding over. He yelped excitedly about the visitors he'd seen and what they'd been wearing and which ones he'd liked the best.

"Do you ever feel scared, Teddy?" asked Zoe as she crouched down beside him.

The little cub tilted his head and thought for a moment. Then he whimpered sadly.

"Oh, it must have been so scary losing your home." Zoe gave him a cuddle. "What do you do to make yourself feel brave?"

Teddy stood in front of her, his head raised and his chest puffed, roaring proudly.

"Yes, you look very brave, standing so tall," replied Zoe. She stood up straight and puffed up her own chest. It did make her feel a bit better. "Thank you, Teddy. That helped a lot." When she gave her

talk, she'd have to remember to be brave
like a tiger.

Later that night when Zoe got into bed,
all of her fears came rushing back. Even
though she'd spent the
evening practising
her talk, she was
still really worried
she'd mess it up.

"Good night,
Zoe," said Lucy,
poking her
head around the
bedroom door.

"I can't sleep,"
said Zoe.

"Oh dear." Lucy
came and sat on the

edge of the bed. "Do you want me to tell you a story? That always helped you fall asleep when you were little."

"Yes please." Zoe closed her eyes and Meep snuggled up beside her.

"Once upon a time there was a girl called Zoe who lived in a zoo…" Lucy began.

And as her mind filled with her mum's story of animal adventures, Zoe finally relaxed and fell fast asleep.

## Chapter Seven
# Bedtime Story

The next morning Zoe woke up feeling a
lot better. As soon as she'd had breakfast,
she and Meep set off to help get things
ready for Endangered Habitat Day. When
they arrived at Higgins Hill, Zoe gasped.
It all looked so lovely! The brightly
coloured banner was draped across the
house and each of the stalls had been

decorated with pictures of the endangered animals.

"Good morning, Zoe! Good morning, Meep!" called Great-Uncle Horace from a small stage in front of the rows of chairs. As usual, Kiki was perched on his shoulder.

"Good morning, Great-Uncle Horace," Zoe called back.

"Could I practise my talk on you?" asked Great-Uncle Horace. "I have some interesting facts about tigers I think you'll like."

"Ooh, yes please!" Zoe sat down in the front row and Meep hopped on to the chair beside her.

"Goo! Goo! Goo!" he cried. Goo was his name for Great-Uncle Horace.

Kiki gave a happy squawk and flew

down to join them.

"Good morning, ladies and gentlemen –
and macaws and mouse lemurs," chuckled
Great-Uncle Horace. "Welcome to the
Endangered Habitat Day. Today I would
like to tell you all about tigers. The first
thing you should know about tigers is that
they *love* to eat. A fully-grown tiger will
eat around five kilograms of meat a day."
Great-Uncle Horace grinned. "That's
around forty hamburgers!"

"Wow!" gasped Zoe.

"I wish I was a tiger and could eat all
that food," sighed Meep.

"But when they live in the wild a tiger
can go for up to two weeks without eating
a thing," continued Great-Uncle Horace.

"I don't think I'd like to be a tiger after
all," muttered Meep.

Great-Uncle Horace went on to talk about Teddy and why he'd needed to rescue him. Listening to how so many tigers had lost their homes made Zoe even more determined to do a good job with her talk. She wondered how the little cub was getting on. Hopefully he'd let the other animals sleep last night!

Great-Uncle Horace finished his talk. Zoe cheered, Meep clapped his paws and Kiki flapped her wings.

"Thank you very much!" he said as he came down from the stage to join them. "I hope my audience tomorrow are just as pleased."

"It was great," replied Zoe.

"How are you feeling about your talk?" asked Great-Uncle Horace. "Are you ready?"

"Yes," replied Zoe, but as she looked at the rows of chairs her tummy began to flutter again. She decided to go and see Teddy to take her mind off it.

When Zoe and Meep got back into the zoo a crowd of people had gathered outside the monkey enclosure. They were all pointing and staring up into the trees.

"Why are the monkeys moving so slowly?" a little boy asked his mum.

Zoe peered inside the enclosure. A spider monkey called Mickey was crawling as slowly as a snail along the ground. Above him a howler monkey called Harry hung from a branch of a tree giving an enormous yawn.

"Why aren't the monkeys running about?" asked Meep, pressing his face to

the enclosure fence.

"I don't know. They look really tired."

"Uh-oh," said Meep.

"Hi Mickey, are you OK?" Zoe said to the spider monkey.

Mickey trudged over. His tail was drooping between his legs.

"What's wrong?" whispered Zoe. "Why do you all look so tired?"

Mickey gave a weary grunt.

"Oh dear," said Zoe.

"What is it?" asked Meep.

"Teddy spent all of last night talking about the moon and stars again."

Mickey grunted again.

"And talking about all the people who came to visit him during the day," Zoe continued. "I'm so sorry you're so tired," she said to Mickey. "I'll go and have another talk with him."

As they hurried over to Teddy's enclosure Zoe noticed that Bertie the elephant was standing with his eyes closed, snoring softly. "Oh dear," she said. "It looks like he kept Bertie awake too."

Teddy didn't seem tired at all. As soon Zoe let herself into his enclosure he came bounding over, chattering excitedly.

"It's lovely to see you too," replied Zoe as Teddy leapt into her lap. "But the other animals are all really tired again from you talking last night."

Teddy gave a sad little yelp.

"It's wonderful that you find it so exciting living here," said Zoe, "but is there any way you can stop getting so excited at night-time?"

Teddy yelped again and patted his head

with his paw.

"My head gets full of thoughts
sometimes too," replied Zoe. She thought
of the night before when her head had
been full of thoughts about her talk. If
Lucy hadn't told her a bedtime story, Zoe

probably wouldn't have slept at all. Then
she had a brilliant idea. "Don't worry,
Teddy, I think I know how I can help."
She gave him a quick cuddle then picked
up Meep. "I'll be back later."

That evening, when the zoo was closed
and all the visitors had gone home, Zoe
set off back to Teddy. A round silver moon
was shining and the sky was full of stars.
Zoe was wearing her cosiest pyjamas and
slippers and holding a sleeping bag. Meep
skipped ahead of her along the winding
footpath.

"We're having a sleepover!" he chattered
excitedly.

Zoe giggled. She was excited too. She
always loved having sleepovers with
her friends but tonight she was having

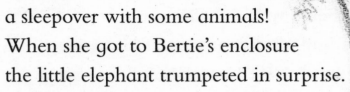

a sleepover with some animals!
When she got to Bertie's enclosure
the little elephant trumpeted in surprise.

"I'm coming to stay the night with
you!" replied Zoe.

Mickey the spider monkey swung
through the trees over to the fence,
chattering down to Zoe.

"I've thought of a way to help you all get a good night's sleep," called Zoe.

Mickey gave a happy shriek. Over in the sea otters' enclosure Nina, Alex, and Sasha splashed the water with excitement.

Zoe went over to a tent by Teddy's enclosure. Lucy had set it up earlier after Zoe had asked if she could stay the night with Teddy to help him settle in. Lucy had also promised to come and check in on Zoe and Meep every couple of hours, just in case they needed anything. Teddy came scampering over to the fence, chattering away about all the zoo visitors he'd seen. Then he remembered that he wasn't supposed to be talking and gave a sad yowl.

"It's OK, Teddy," said Zoe. "I know how to get your thoughts out of your head without keeping everyone awake."

Teddy looked at her hopefully.

"I'm going to show you how to turn them into a bedtime story," said Zoe. "That way, you'll get them out of your head *and* help the other animals fall asleep."

Bertie gave an excited trumpet, the monkeys squealed and the sea otters splashed about joyfully. Meep ran between each of the enclosures, his long tail bobbing up and down.

"We're having a story! We're having a story!" he exclaimed.

Teddy yelped at Zoe.

"Don't worry, all you have to do is
tell me your thoughts and I'll turn them
into a story," replied Zoe. She sat on her
pillow just outside the tent. "Settle down
everyone, it's time for your bedtime story."

Meep scampered into the tent and lay
down.

Teddy started to chatter quietly, telling Zoe what he'd seen that day.

"Once upon a time, there was a very neat and tidy man, with very shiny shoes," began Zoe. She giggled. "I think he's talking about Mr Pinch!" she whispered to Meep.

Teddy continued to chatter.

"One day, the man with the shiny shoes went on an adventure all the way to a place called India," said Zoe.

Bertie gave a contented sigh and lay down on his side.

Teddy continued telling Zoe his thoughts.

"When he arrived in India the man with the shiny shoes went to a forest in a place called Bengal. There were bad men in the forest," said Zoe. "They wanted to chop down the trees to build farms on the land."

Over in the monkey enclosure, there was the rustle of leaves. Zoe looked up and saw that the monkeys were settling into the trees, getting ready to go to sleep.

Teddy paced up and down, still telling Zoe his thoughts.

"But the man with the shiny shoes was very brave," continued Zoe. "He told the men they couldn't have the land and he made them go away."

Over in the sea otters' enclosure the sound of splashing quietened, and Zoe could see Nina, Alex and Sasha floating on their backs in the moonlight. Teddy yawned and gave a quiet little growl.

"The tigers were so happy that the man with the shiny shoes had saved them they made him their king," said Zoe. She couldn't help grinning as she thought of Mr Pinch being king of the tigers. "They gave him a shiny golden crown and a long velvet cloak. And they called him King Pinch." Zoe waited for Teddy to tell her some more of his thoughts, but the little tiger was silent. She looked over to his enclosure and saw him curled in a ball, fast asleep! Zoe tiptoed over to

Bertie's enclosure. The little elephant was fast asleep too. And so were the monkeys, and the sea otters.

"My plan worked!" whispered Zoe, as she went back to the tent. But Meep was fast asleep too! Zoe snuggled inside her sleeping bag and gave a contented smile.

## Chapter Eight
# Endangered Habitat Day

When Zoe woke the next morning, she poked her head out of the tent and looked around. She really hoped the animals had slept well! Over in the elephant enclosure Bertie was using his trunk to give himself a wash. The monkeys were shrieking happily and swinging through the trees and the sea otters were splashing

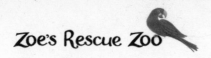

around in their pool. Zoe grinned. They
all looked as if they'd had a good night's
sleep. Meep sat up and rubbed his eyes.

"Is it morning?" he asked.

"Yes, it is."

"But I didn't hear
Teddy talking."

"That's because he fell asleep." Zoe got
out of the tent and looked into Teddy's
enclosure. The little cub was still curled up,
fast asleep.

"He must have been tired out after all
the talking he's been doing," giggled Zoe.

Just then Jess arrived to feed the sea otters their breakfast.

"Good morning, Zoe," she called. "How was your sleepover?"

"It was great," replied Zoe.

"Nina, Alex and Sasha seem to have enjoyed it too," smiled Jess. "They seem very happy!"

Zoe grinned. If only Jess knew the real reason! While Jess was feeding the sea otters Zoe went over to say good morning to Bertie.

As soon as Bertie saw her he trumpeted joyfully.

"I'm so happy my story helped you sleep well," said Zoe.

Mickey the spider monkey scampered over to the fence of his enclosure, chattering happily.

"You're very welcome," replied Zoe.

Just then Teddy woke up and came
running over to the fence.

"Good morning, Teddy," called Zoe.

Teddy yelped happily.

Bertie gave a worried grunt.

"No, I won't be able to sleep here every
night," said Zoe.

Mickey's tail dropped and he gave an
anxious squeak.

"Don't worry," said Zoe. "I know how
to stop Teddy talking at night – without
me needing to sleep over." She went
to Teddy's enclosure and let herself in
with her pendant. The little cub came
bounding over, chattering excitedly.

"I'm really glad you enjoyed my story,"
said Zoe. "You helped the other animals
to sleep too." She sat down and Teddy

leapt into her lap. "I have a plan. Tonight, when I'm not here, I want you to make all of your thoughts into a story inside your head."

Teddy yelped.

"No, don't tell the story at night, tell it to me in the morning. Then I'll tell the story to the other animals tomorrow evening before I go back home and you'll all be able to sleep."

Teddy chattered happily and when the other animals heard Zoe's plan, they were all really happy too.

"Phew!" said Zoe as she packed up her sleeping bag and picked up Meep. That was one problem solved. But soon it would be time for Endangered Habitat Day and she would have to give her talk!

Once Zoe had eaten breakfast and gotten
dressed, she set off for
Higgins Hill with
Meep perched on
her shoulder. It was
another lovely sunny
day and the zoo
was bustling with
visitors. Zoe
knew that this
was a very good
thing. The more
people who came
to Endangered
Habitat Day, the
more money they
would raise to
help the animals.
But the thought of having to get up and

speak in front of so many people made her legs feel wobbly.

When Zoe got to the hill people were crowding around the stalls, chatting to the keepers and looking at the animals. A lady was doing face-painting and lots

of the children had stripes like Teddy's on their faces. Sally, the manager of the café, had a stall too. She was selling cupcakes with stripy frosting.

"Would you like a tiger cake, Zoe?" she called.

Zoe shook her head. She was way too
nervous to eat anything. She carried
on walking around the displays until
she found Great-Uncle Horace. He was
standing in front of a giant map of the
world. Kiki was perched on top of the
map, squawking happily at the crowd.

"Win a special prize if you can point to
a country that tigers come from," called
Great-Uncle Horace.

A little girl pointed to Africa.

"I'm afraid tigers don't come from any
of the countries in Africa," said Great-
Uncle Horace. "But don't worry, that's a
common mistake. Maybe my niece Zoe
can help you?" he smiled at Zoe.

"Of course." Zoe went over to the girl
and helped her find India on the map.

"Congratulations!" cried Great-Uncle

Horace and he gave the girl a cuddly
tiger toy.

Just then Mr Pinch arrived, muttering under his breath. "All these people everywhere, making the place look messy."

"Don't worry, Mr Pinch," said Great-Uncle Horace. "It's time for us to give our talks. Maybe you could get everyone to sit in the chairs and then they'll all look neat and tidy."

"Excellent!" exclaimed Mr Pinch. "Can everyone please take a seat," he called to the crowd. "The talks are about to begin."

Zoe's tummy churned. There were so many people that there weren't enough seats and some of them had to stand!

Great-Uncle Horace strode up on to the stage and Mark joined him with Teddy on a lead.

Everyone clapped and cheered when

they saw the little tiger cub. Teddy started happily chattering back at them.

"Hello everyone, welcome to Endangered Habitat Day!" said Great-Uncle Horace. "I would now like to introduce you to our newest arrival at the zoo – if he'll let me!" he chuckled as Teddy kept yelping excitedly. "This is Teddy, and he's come all the way from Bengal in India," continued Great-Uncle Horace. As he went on to tell the crowd his interesting tiger facts the words all blurred together in Zoe's head. What if she forgot what to say? What if she messed up her talk? Meep scampered on to her shoulder. She couldn't mess it up. Other mouse lemurs like Meep needed her help to keep their habitats safe.

"But tigers like Teddy aren't the only

animals whose homes are endangered," continued Great-Uncle Horace. "Many other animals are facing extinction because of this. One of those animals is the mouse lemur.

Ladies and gentlemen, I would now like to welcome my great-niece Zoe to the stage. Zoe is going to tell you all about the endangered habitats of mouse lemurs like her special friend Meep."

As the audience clapped and cheered Zoe went on to the stage, her heart pounding.

## Chapter Nine
# Once Upon a Time

Zoe gazed out at the audience. Everyone had fallen silent and they were all staring up at her. Even Teddy wasn't making a sound as they waited for her to speak.

"Hello, everyone." Zoe's voice came out like a little mouse's squeak.

"I can't hear you," someone called.

"Neither can I," said another.

Zoe remembered what Teddy had said about how to be brave. She stood up tall and puffed out her chest. "Hello, everyone." Her voice was much clearer this time. But now her mind had gone completely blank. Zoe tried and tried but she couldn't remember how her talk was meant to begin.

Teddy let out an encouraging little yelp.

"I wonder what that tiger just said," said a little boy in the front row.

Zoe knew exactly what Teddy was saying. He was wishing her good luck with her story. But Zoe wasn't telling a story, she was supposed to be giving a talk. Unless… She remembered how well the animals had listened last night when she told them a story. Maybe she could do the same now. She had to say something.

"Once upon a time," she began. "There was a little mouse lemur named Meep."

Meep hopped down from her shoulder and scampered to the front of the stage. The audience cheered. Seeing their smiling faces made Zoe feel braver. "Meep lived on an island near Africa called Madagascar," continued Zoe. "It was a beautiful island, full of unusual plants and wildlife that can't be found anywhere else on earth."

Meep stood on his hind legs proudly.

"Meep and the other mouse lemurs lived in a forest in Madagascar and they loved having fun and climbing trees," said Zoe.

Meep chattered excitedly and scampered up on to Zoe's shoulder as if he was climbing a tree.

"Meep and his family lived in a cosy hole inside one of the trees," continued Zoe. "His friends lived in other trees nearby and they loved to play together and go on a hunt for food."

At the mention of food, Meep ran in a circle chasing his tail. The audience started to laugh and clap.

"But then something really sad happened…" Zoe continued. The audience fell totally silent. Even Mr Pinch looked really interested. "Some men came to the forest and they started cutting down the trees."

"Oh no!" gasped a little girl. Meep pulled a sad face and his ears and tail drooped.

"They didn't stop chopping the trees until they'd all gone," continued Zoe.

"But why?" called the girl.

"They wanted to make farms on the land," explained Zoe. "So poor Meep lost his home."

"This is a really sad story," said the little girl.

"Don't worry, it has a happy ending." Zoe picked up Meep. "My Great-Uncle Horace flew to Madagascar in his hot air balloon and he rescued Meep and brought him back here."

"Hurray!" cheered the girl.

Meep clapped his paws together.

"But there are lots of mouse lemurs just like Meep who might not be so lucky," said Zoe. "Unless we do something to help."

"Mum, can we do something to help?" cried the little girl. Her mum nodded.

"I want to help too," called a boy.

And then everyone was calling out, "Me too!"

Zoe grinned. "You can help by donating some money to help save wild animal habitats." She pointed to the collection box by the stage. Meep ran over to it and jumped up and down. Everyone cheered.

"Thank you for listening to my story," said Zoe and the crowd all cheered again, loudly. As Zoe left the stage Meep scampered up on to her shoulder.

"I loved your story. Especially the bit about hunting for food," he chattered into her ear.

"Thank you for helping me tell it," giggled Zoe.

"I hope the people will help save the animals," said Meep.

"I think they will," said Zoe. "Look." She pointed to a long queue of people waiting to put money in the collection box, which Mark was holding out with a smile.

Meep grinned but then his face fell. "Uh-oh."

Zoe turned to see Mr Pinch marching

over to them and her heart sank. He was
probably going to tell Zoe off for letting
Meep run about on the stage.
But to her surprise he took a
handkerchief from his pocket
and dabbed at his eyes. "That
was a very good story,"
he sniffed.

Then he took some money from his
pocket. "I would like to make a donation
to help save the mouse lemurs' habitat."

"Thank you, Mr Pinch!" exclaimed
Zoe.

"Yes well, I can't stand here and chat all
day," he muttered. "I have tidying to do."

"Wow!" exclaimed Zoe as Mr Pinch
went marching off towards the collection
box.

"Wowee!" shrieked Meep.

"Well done, Zoe," boomed Great-Uncle
Horace as he came striding over with
Teddy. The little tiger jumped up at Zoe,
roaring with joy. "It was such a good idea
to tell a story instead of giving a talk,"
continued Great-Uncle Horace.

"Thank you," replied Zoe, bending
down to cuddle Teddy. "And thank *you* for

giving me the idea," she whispered in the cub's ear. Teddy started chattering away and a crowd of people gathered round.

As they all petted the little tiger Zoe smiled. The zoo certainly was a lot livelier since Teddy had come to live there. She wondered if the next animal to come to the Rescue Zoo would be as chatty and friendly. She really hoped so!

If you enjoyed Teddy's story,
look out for:

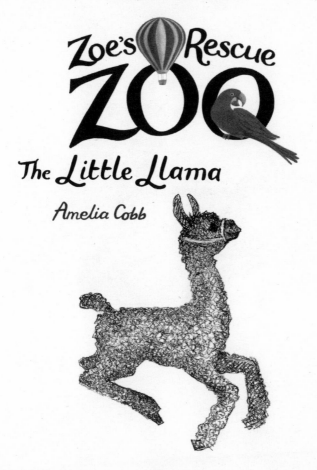

Zoe's Rescue
ZOO

The Little Llama

Amelia Cobb

nosy
crow

# Chapter One
# **Very Special Guests**

Zoe Parker finished her packed lunch and rushed out into the playground.

"Is it snowing yet?" called her friend Priti from behind her.

"No!" sighed Zoe. The weather forecast had been saying it might snow all week but so far there hadn't been a single flake, despite it being freezing cold. Zoe and her friends were so excited about playing in the snow! Still, Zoe did have something to look forward to. This afternoon her Great-Uncle Horace was coming to give a talk at her school. It was almost time for the school's big winter show and Great-Uncle Horace had agreed to help them with it this year!

Zoe's Great-Uncle Horace was a famous explorer and he travelled all over the world rescuing animals who were lost, injured or endangered. He brought the animals back to live at the Rescue Zoo. Zoe lived at the zoo too, with her mum, Lucy, who was the zoo vet.

"It's so cold!" said Zoe's friend Jack, coming out to join the girls. "Shall we play chase to warm up?"

"Good idea!" grinned Zoe.

But before they could begin their game she heard the sound of a car horn playing a musical tune. Zoe's eyes sparkled. There was only one car horn she knew that sounded like that and it belonged to Great-Uncle Horace! She spun round to face the school gates. Sure enough, Great-Uncle Horace's cherry-red car was pulling up outside.

"It's my great-uncle!" she cried.

"Cool car!" exclaimed Priti.

Great-Uncle Horace's car was a convertible, which meant that the roof could come down. But the roof wasn't down today because it was far too cold. A wooden trailer was attached to the back of the car. Zoe felt butterflies flutter in her tummy. Great-Uncle Horace usually used the trailer to transport animals in. Had he brought an animal with him to *school*?

"Come on, let's go and see him!" said
Zoe, and she and her friends hurried over
to the school gates.

The school caretaker opened the gates
and Great-Uncle Horace drove inside and
parked next to the playing field.

"Zoe, my dear!" he cried as he got out
of the car. "It's so wonderful to see you.
Brrrr, it's a bit chilly though!"

"It's so good to see you too!" said Zoe,
giving him a big hug. Then she heard a
weird humming sound coming from the
trailer.

"What's in the trailer?" she asked.

"A special guest," replied Great-Uncle
Horace with a twinkle in his eyes. "I've
just collected her, so I thought I'd bring
her along to join in the fun!"

"I thought *you* were the special guest."
Zoe giggled.

"Well, yes, I suppose I am." Great-Uncle
Horace grinned. "But this guest is even
more special!"

# Zoe's Rescue Zoo

**Look out for more
amazing animal adventures
at the Rescue Zoo!**

# The Secret Rescuers

If you enjoyed this book,
we think you'll love The Secret Rescuers!

# The Rescue Princesses

## Look out for another AMAZING series from Nosy Crow!

Friendship, animals and
secret royal adventures!

# Look out for another AMAZING series from Nosy Crow!

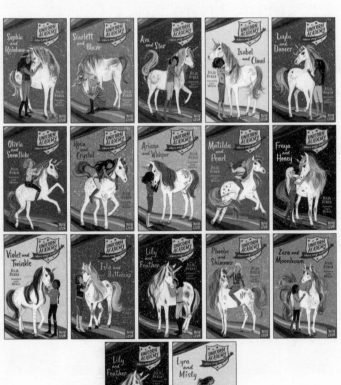